Bamboo & Friends
The Dragonfly

by Felicia Law
illustrated by Claire Philpott

Editor: Jacqueline A. Wolfe
Page Production: Tracy Davies
Creative Director: Keith Griffin
Editorial Director: Carol Jones
Managing Editor: Catherine Neitge

First American edition published in 2006 by
Picture Window Books
5115 Excelsior Boulevard
Suite 232
Minneapolis, MN 55416
877-845-8392
www.picturewindowbooks.com

Copyright © 2004 by Allegra Publishing Limited
Unit 13/15 Quayside Lodge
William Morris Way
Townmead Road
London SW6 2UZ
UK

Printed in the United States of America.

Library of Congress Cataloging-in-Publication Data
Law, Felicia.
The dragonfly / by Felicia Law ; illustrated by Claire
Philpott.— 1st American ed.
p. cm. — (Bamboo & friends)
Summary: Velvet tries to persuade Bamboo not to be afraid
of dragonflies.
ISBN 1-4048-1302-0 (hardcover)
[1. Rain forests—Fiction. 2. Pandas—Fiction. 3. Zebras—Fiction.
4. Birds—Fiction. 5. Dragonflies—Fiction.] I. Philpott, Claire, ill.
II. Title. III. Series.
PZ7.L41835Dra 2005
[E]—dc22   2005008723

Bamboo, Velvet, and Beak sit on their log in the middle of the magical forest, just as they always do.

4

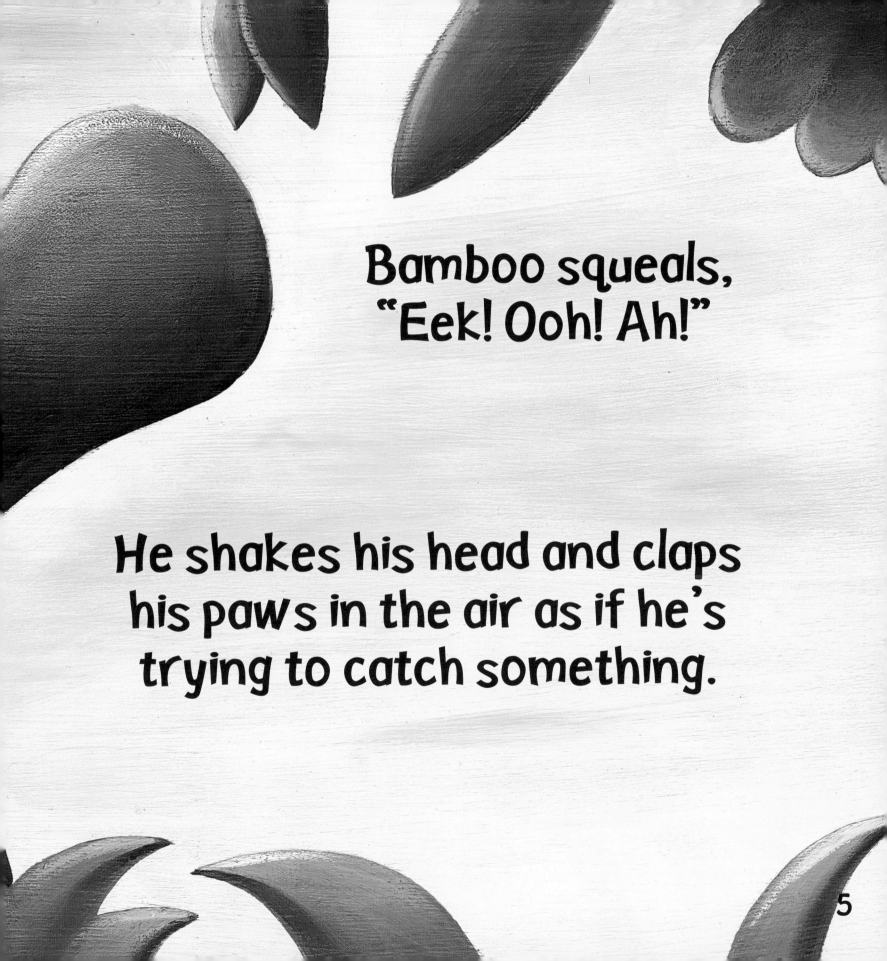

Bamboo squeals,
"Eek! Ooh! Ah!"

He shakes his head and claps
his paws in the air as if he's
trying to catch something.

5

Bamboo swipes the air
again yelling, "Shoo!"

"What's up?" asks Beak.
"Are you having
a nightmare?"

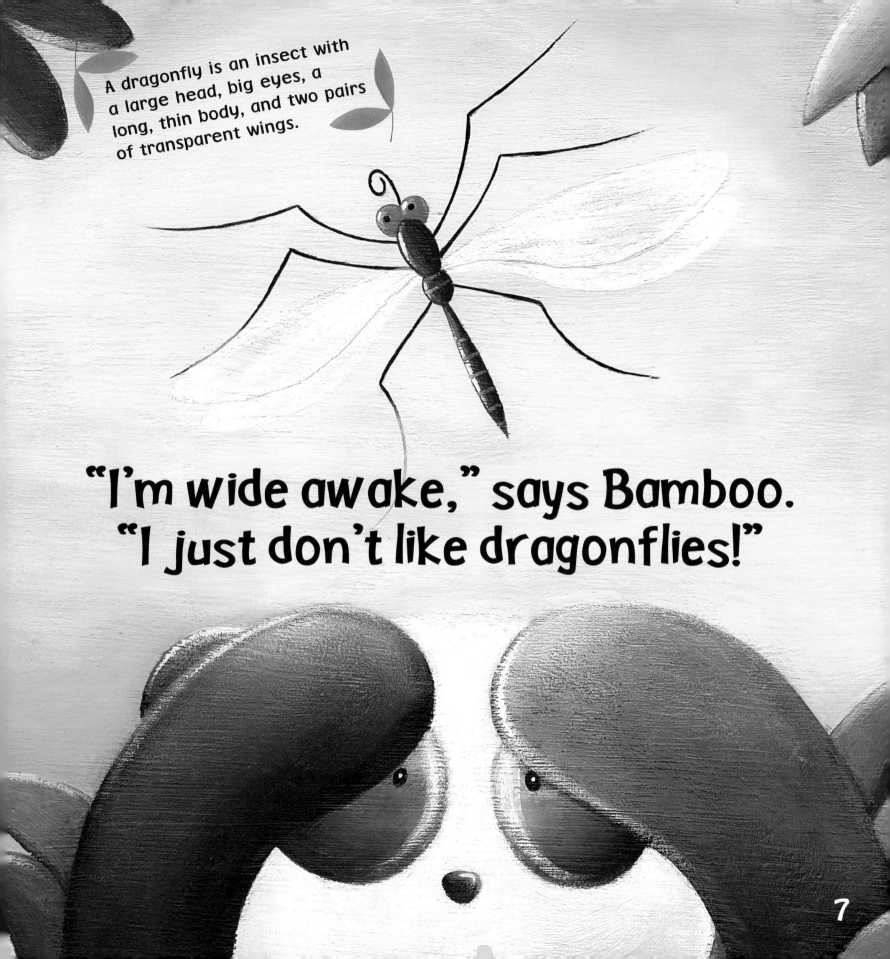

A dragonfly is an insect with a large head, big eyes, a long, thin body, and two pairs of transparent wings.

"I'm wide awake," says Bamboo. "I just don't like dragonflies!"

7

Bamboo shudders and says, "I don't like spiders either, but I dislike dragonflies the most."

"It won't hurt you," says Velvet calmly. "Look! It's so fragile!"

"Its wings are so light and delicate
you can almost see through them.

Its legs are so thin they're hardly there," says Velvet.

Dragonflies are harmless to humans and animals.

11

"And it's a million times smaller than you," adds Beak.

Dragonflies only grow to be a few inches long.

"Ugh! I don't care!"
says Bamboo.
"I don't like
creepy crawlies."

13

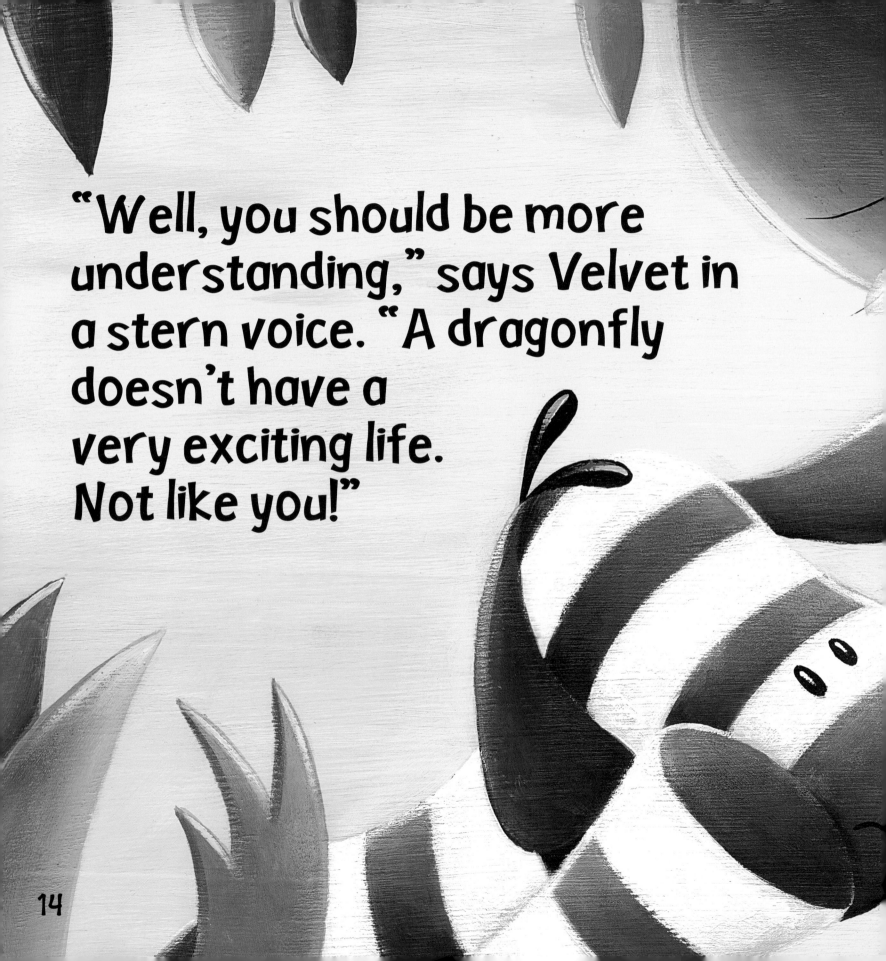

"Well, you should be more understanding," says Velvet in a stern voice. "A dragonfly doesn't have a very exciting life. Not like you!"

She keeps one eye on the insect that's circling around Bamboo's head and whispers, "And it only lives for a month."

15

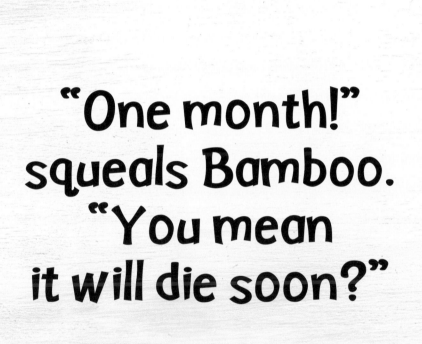

"One month!"
squeals Bamboo.
"You mean
it will die soon?"

"Shh!" says Velvet.
"It probably
doesn't know."

"Or," adds Beak, "it may get eaten by a frog."

Some frogs take less than a second to roll out their long, sticky tongue, catch an insect, and roll it back into their mouths.

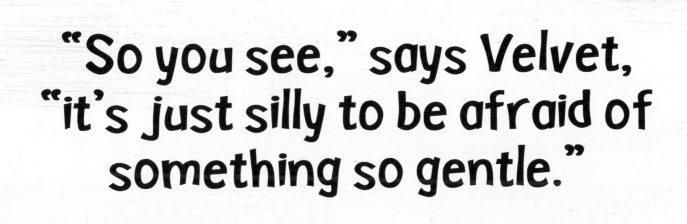

"So you see," says Velvet, "it's just silly to be afraid of something so gentle."

"I'm sorry," says Bamboo. "I'll try to be nicer to dragonflies from now on."

"AND spiders!"
warns Velvet.
"They have feelings, too."

23

Fun Facts

- Frogs eat almost any live prey they can find—insects, snails, spiders, or worms.

- Frogs swallow their food whole because they cannot chew.

- Giant pandas are usually quiet, but they can bleat. They sound more like a sheep or a goat than a growling bear.

- Some giant pandas in zoos have lived for as many as 35 years. Scientists are not sure how old pandas get when they live in the wild.

- Most zebras live to be about 28 years old.

- Young zebras spend time running and play-fighting. They also like to nibble the hair on each other's back and neck.

- Dragonflies eat mosquitoes and other small insects but are harmless to people.

- In places where it doesn't get very hot or cold, a dragonfly may spend several years in the larval stage. Once it becomes an adult, it lives for only one or two months.

- Dragonfly wings are always spread flat, even when the dragonfly is resting.

On the Web

FactHound offers a safe, fun way to find Internet sites related to this book. All of the sites on FactHound have been researched by our staff.

Here's how:

1. Visit www.facthound.com

2. Type in this special code for age-appropriate sites: 1404813020

3. Click on the FETCH IT button.

Your trusty FactHound will fetch the best sites for you!

Look for all of the books about Bamboo & Friends: